FIRE RESCUE

EMERGENCY VEHICLES

Deborah Chancellor

This edition 2015

First published in 2012 by
Franklin Watts
338 Euston Road
London, NW1 3BH

Franklin Watts Australia
Level 17/207 Kent Street
Sydney, NSW 2000

A CIP catalogue record for this book
is available from the British Library

Dewey Classification: 628.9'259
ISBN: 978 1 4451 3814 5

Printed in China

Series editors: Adrian Cole/Amy Stephenson
Editor: Sarah Ridley
Art direction: Peter Scoulding
Designer: Steve Prosser
Picture researcher: Diana Morris

Franklin Watts is a division of Hachette
Children's Books, an Hachette UK company.
www.hachette.co.uk

WHOOSH!

Contents

Sound and light

A fire engine is coming! The noisy **siren** tells drivers to move out of the way.

BARP! BARP!

The engine carries special tools and **equipment**.

WHOOOOO! WHOOOOO!

Bright lights flash to warn people that the fire engine is racing to an emergency.

Siren

Bell

Sky high

The long ladder on this engine stretches up and up to save people from fires in tall buildings.

CRANK! CRANK! WHIRRR! WHIRRR!

Firefighters climb the ladder to get close to the fire. They use a hose to blast water at the blaze.

The ladder is strong and safe.

Water

City speed

Shiny fire motorbikes can roar through crowded streets, speeding past traffic to the scene of a blaze.

Big **panniers** carry fire fighting equipment and a first-aid kit.

Off-road

This off-road fire truck reaches **wildfires** in far off places. It has a four-wheel drive and tough tyres, to help it move over bumpy ground.

BUMP!

Inside the cab, a **sat nav** helps the crew find the fire.

The fire truck carries a tank of water to put out leaping flames.

THUD!

BUMP!

Air attack

A fire plane attacks big wildfires from the air. It carries a tank and spraying equipment.

The plane scoops up water to fill its tanks.

WHOOSH!

EEEOOWW!

WHOOSH!

The plane dumps water on the fire below.

Up and away

This fire helicopter is on its way to an emergency. It dips a special bucket into the lake to fill it up with water.

CHUPPA!

WHUPPA!

WHUPPA!

CHUPPA!

WHOOSHH!

The noisy fire helicopter hovers above the fire, dropping water on the flames.

Fire express

In some countries, special trains fight fires on railways, in tunnels and near the track.

Water tank

PSSHHH!
PSSHHH!

Fire hose

A strong **locomotive** pulls heavy tanks, pumps and **power generators** to the scene of the fire.

PSSHHH!
PSSHHH!

Pump and spray

The fireboat has rushed to a burning ship. It pumps water from under the fireboat and aims it at the flames.

SPLASH!

WHOOSH!

A fireboat tests out its water jets in Hong Kong harbour.

Water jets shoot out of nozzles.

WHOOOSHH!

WHOOSH!

Crash site

An airport **crash tender** smashes through barriers to reach a burning plane on the runway.

≥WHOOSHHH!

FFSSSTTT

Powerful pumps spray foam and water at the fire.

A mechanical arm lifts a hose above the flames.

SPLASH!

EMERGENCY SERVICES

16

Glossary

crash tender
a fire engine that is specially designed to fight airport fires

equipment
the things you need to do something

locomotive
the engine that pulls a train

nozzle
the spout at the end of a hose

panniers
boxes and bags on the back of a bike

power generator
machinery that makes electricity

sat nav
a piece of equipment that uses information received from a satellite to give directions

siren
a loud hooting or wailing sound

two-way radio
a radio set you use to talk to somebody far away

wildfire
a fire that destroys forests and other plant life

Quiz

1. Why do fire motorbikes have flashing lights?

2. Why do fire engines carry ladders?

3. Why do fire engines need sirens?

4. How do fire helicopters collect water?

5. What are fire trains for?

6. What is an airport crash tender?

Answers:

1. Flashing lights make fire motorbikes easy to see in traffic.

2. Ladders help firefighters reach tall buildings.

3. A fire engine's sirens warn vehicles to slow down.

4. Fire helicopters use buckets to scoop up water from the sea, rivers and lakes.

5. Fire trains put out fires in tunnels and by the track.

6. An airport crash tender is a special fire engine at an airport.

23

Index

BEEEEP!